Disney
Beauty
AND THE
Beast

EGMONT
We bring stories to life

First published in Great Britain in 2017
by Egmont UK Limited,
The Yellow Building, 1 Nicholas Road,
London W11 4AN

© 2017 Disney Enterprises, Inc.

ISBN 978 1 4052 8822 4
67790/4
Printed in Italy.

ID EGM17GLO0422-01

Once upon a time, there lived a young prince. He was handsome but heartless. He cared only for outer beauty and material things. The Prince surrounded himself with priceless paintings, extravagant riches and beautiful things. His greatest pleasures in life were showing off these treasures and boasting his wealth by hosting many extravagant parties, attended by the most privileged members of high society.

And his life would have continued in much the same way – dancing his days away and caring for nothing – had it not been for one fateful night.

On that evening, the Prince threw an elaborate masquerade ball. The guests wore white, their faces hidden behind masks. The Prince was also dressed up, but his mask had been painted on by servants, with feathers of delicate blues and golden tones framing his eyes.

As the festivities wore on, the Prince surveyed the beautiful subjects before him. He danced with one maiden after another until suddenly, there was a knock on the ballroom door.

A moment later, a great gust of wind ripped through the open windows, causing the candles to flicker and the ladies to let out startled screams.

Furious at the interruption, the Prince turned to behold who had caused this disturbance, only to find an old beggar woman. Her face was wrinkled and her skin covered in spots. She stood hunched over.

The Prince demanded an explanation. Falling to her knees, the old woman held out a single rose, which she offered in return for shelter from the bitter storm. But the Prince was unmoved and waved the old woman away.

The Prince ordered two of his servants to usher the woman out. "You should not be deceived by appearances," the beggar warned, "for beauty is found within."

The Prince threw back his head and laughed cruelly. Turning his back on the woman, he heard a collective gasp. He spun around just as the room burst into light!

Where once a horrible hag stood, there was now a beautiful enchantress. She floated magically in the air. This time it was the Prince who kneeled. He had been put to a test ... and he had failed.

"Please," he cried, and he begged for forgiveness. But his words, the Enchantress knew, were as hollow as his heart. With a flick of her wrist, she cast her spell. The air filled with magic and when it had cleared, the Prince was gone. In his place stood a hideous beast – a beast as terrifying and cruel-looking on the outside as the Prince had been on the inside.

With the gift of an enchanted rose, the Enchantress told him his fate. The Prince would remain in his beastly form until he learned to love and found someone who could do what he had not – look deeper than appearances and love him for who he was, not what he appeared to be. And if the last petal fell from the rose before that day arrived, he would remain a beast ... forever.

Nearby, in a small village, lived a kind, intelligent and independent young woman named Belle, whose high spirit was matched only by her exceeding beauty. She opened the door to her cottage and stepped outside. Belle had lived in the same small home in the same small village for almost her whole life. Every day was the same as the day before. She saw the same people. She did the same things. But she yearned for adventure.

Belle sighed. If she stayed in the village, she knew the greatest adventure she would ever find would be in the pages of her favourite book. And with that thought, she headed into the village, wondering what the future might yet hold.

While Belle was generous of heart and fair-minded, another resident of the village was quite the opposite: a vain and arrogant man named Gaston. Gaston loved adventures almost as much as he loved himself. He knew that all the men in the village wanted to be him and all the ladies wanted to marry him.

Belle was the most beautiful girl in the village. That, Gaston reasoned, made her the best. And he, being the most handsome man in the village, deserved the best.

However, no matter how hard Gaston tried to win Belle over, she wanted nothing to do with him. Every attempt he made was met with polite yet firm rejection. Despite Belle's clear disinterest, Gaston was determined to claim her as his own – no matter what it took.

When Belle returned to the cottage, she heard music coming from her father's workshop. Maurice made beautiful music boxes that depicted exotic lands. Belle loved to hold them and imagine she was travelling to far-off places.

On that particular day, Maurice was putting the finishing touches on a delicate music box. Inside the box were three small figures – a family composed of a father, mother, and baby girl. Belle smiled sadly. She knew these figures to be her family as it had once been.

"Tell me more about her," Belle said, walking over to stand behind her father.

Maurice looked up. "Your mother was … fearless," he said. "To know anything more, you just have to look in the mirror."

Belle smiled softly, her heart touched by her father's words. Maurice set the last gear into its proper place and then closed the lid on the finished music box. This piece would be his greatest work at the market, where he journeyed every year to sell his creations.

Belle helped her father load his wares into the cart. Lifting her hand in the air, she waved goodbye to her father. Maurice waved back and then steered their horse, Philippe, and the cart onto the path.

With her father off to the market, Belle resumed her daily tasks and chores, grabbing her basket of laundry and heading into the village square. Belle had devised a contraption that made doing laundry much easier. While the clothes soaked in a barrel pulled by a mule, she opened her book. As she sat at the edge of the *laverie* reading, a young girl approached, asking what Belle was doing. Belle invited the girl to sit with her and soon Belle was teaching the girl how to read.

"What on earth are you doing?" the school's headmaster shouted.

Hearing the angry words, Belle looked up from her book. The headmaster was staring down at her with a scowl on his face. "Girls don't read," he barked.

The headmaster was joined by the scornful fishmonger and other townspeople. They were outraged by Belle teaching the young girl. In an instant, they pulled Belle's laundry barrel from the water and turned it upside down over the street, spilling all of Belle's things onto the dusty ground. Having interrupted Belle's lesson with the young girl, the townspeople were smug, but Belle was furious with her neighbours' narrow-mindedness and old-fashioned thinking.

As she neared her cottage, she was approached by Gaston, who continued to seek her favour, practically demanding she marry him.

"I'm sorry, but I will never marry you, Gaston," she answered again. Then, without another word, she walked up the front steps of her cottage, marched inside and slammed the door.

When she was sure Gaston had left, Belle opened the door. Making her way to the top of the hill that overlooked the village, she sighed. Why couldn't anyone understand her? She wanted more than Gaston or this small town could ever offer. She wanted an adventure.

Meanwhile, Maurice was lost in the woods. As lightning flashed in the sky, Philippe whinnied in fright and tugged on his harness.

"It will be all right, Philippe," Maurice said. But his voice was shaking. Just then, another bolt of lightning struck. It hit a tree right in front of them, splitting it in half and blocking their way. Maurice had no choice. He turned Philippe down an older, overgrown path.

They hadn't gone far before Maurice knew he had made a big mistake. Even though it was summer, it began to snow. And then he heard a howl.

Looking around, Maurice saw they were surrounded by a pack of hungry wolves. The animals snarled and began to come closer. Maurice leapt from the cart onto Philippe's back with no time to spare, racing to escape the pack of wolves nipping at their heels.

Just when Maurice was sure they were doomed, a gate appeared in front of them. It opened and Philippe raced through. Seconds later, it slammed shut, stopping the wolves in their tracks.

Looking ahead, Maurice saw a huge castle. Though he was unsure where he was, or whether he would be welcome in this ominous place, Maurice left Philippe at the stable and went towards the castle.

After making his way up the front steps, Maurice took a deep breath and knocked on the door.

The door creaked open. "Hello?" Maurice called out, peering in. "Anyone home?"

No one answered.

Shivering, Maurice stepped inside. "Forgive me," he said. "I don't mean to intrude. I need shelter from the storm. Hello?" Still no one answered.

Maurice looked around at the huge room. It was hard to see anything in the dim light, but he did notice a coat rack. He took off his hat and coat and hung them on the rack. Then, with a shrug, he moved further into the seemingly abandoned castle.

Behind him, unseen by the weary traveller, the coat rack came to life and shook the snow off Maurice's jacket.

Hearing the sound of a crackling fire, Maurice made his way down a hall. He stopped in front of a large pair of open doors. Through them, he saw the fire roaring. He quickly made his way inside and reached his hands towards the flames. He let out a long breath as warmth flooded through him.

Maurice hadn't been standing there long when he smelled something delicious wafting through another set of doors. Following his nose, he found himself in a dining room.

A long table had been set with plates of steaming food. "Do you mind ...? I'm just going to help myself ..." he called out to the unseen host of the dinner.

Reaching out, Maurice picked up a piece of bread and a hunk of cheese. Then a cup of tea slid into his hand to help wash it all down.

"Mom said I wasn't supposed to move because it might be scary."

Maurice yelped. The teacup had just talked to him! Looking down, he saw a small face in the china staring up at him. Letting out another yelp, Maurice put down the cup and ran.

Pushing open the castle's front door, Maurice hurried down the steps and fetched Philippe. He paused as he passed the glistening white rosebushes. Every time he went on a trip, Belle asked him to bring home a red rose. These weren't red, but they were beautiful. He was sure Belle would love one. He reached out and plucked a rose.

"Those are *mine*!"

The words echoed off the castle walls. Instantly, Maurice began to shake. Before him, a giant beast appeared out of the shadows. It walked on its hind legs and wore a long, tattered cloak. Maurice stumbled backward. The rose fell from his hand.

"You entered my home," the creature said, dropping to all fours and circling Maurice, "and *this* is how I am repaid."

Maurice tried to apologise, but before he could get the words out, the creature lifted him off the ground.

"I know how to deal with thieves," the Beast snarled. Then, with a growl, he turned and headed back into the castle, dragging Maurice along with him.

Back in the village, Belle was up early. She was tending the garden when out of nowhere, Philippe galloped to the front gate. He was alone, breathing heavily, and his sides were dirty and soaked with sweat.

Rushing over, Belle saw that the horse's bridle was ripped and he had several scratches along his side. He let out a sad little whicker.

Something was very wrong.

Quickly, Belle put a saddle on Philippe's back and threw on a new bridle. She needed him to take her to her father.

Belle and Philippe raced through the forest. When they reached the overturned cart, Belle urged Philippe on with determination in her eyes. A few minutes later, they arrived at the castle. Taking a deep breath, Belle walked through the doors, knowing her father must be inside.

As Belle's eyes adjusted to the dark, she thought she heard whispering.
"But what if she's the one?" a voice said. "The one who will break
the spell?"

"Who said that?" Belle asked, turning towards the noise.
No one answered. Instead, Belle heard someone coughing.
"Papa!" she cried, running towards the sound.

Belle grabbed a nearby candelabra and raced up a grand staircase and through the castle. Reaching the very top of a smaller staircase, she realised she was in a prison tower. Through a single door made of iron, Belle heard the coughing again.

"Papa?" Belle called out. "Is that you?"

"Belle?" Maurice's muffled voice answered. "How did you find me?"

Racing over, Belle dropped to her knees in front of the door. "Oh, Papa," she said, reaching her fingers through the narrow openings in the iron. "We need to get you home."

To her surprise, Maurice did not agree. He urged her to flee. "Belle, this castle is alive!" he cried. "You must get away before he finds you!"

"He?" Belle repeated.

Suddenly, a roar filled the tower.

Belle shrank against the prison door as a deep rumbling voice came out of the shadows. "Who are *you*?" the voice said. "How did you get in here?"

"I've come for my father," Belle said bravely. "Release him."

"Your father is a thief," the voice replied, sounding closer.

"Liar!" Belle shouted. Her father was a loving and kind man, not a thief.

"He stole a rose!" the voice roared.

Belle's breath caught in her throat. She knew the only reason her father would have taken the rose was to give it to her. This was all her fault.

"Punish me, not him," Belle said. Her father shouted in protest.

Belle demanded her captor come out of the shadows. When he stepped into the light, Belle gasped.

Standing in front of her was a huge creature. It had horns and fangs, and its entire body was covered in golden-brown fur. It stood upright, its two front paws clenched into fists. The word *beast* flashed in her mind as she gazed upon the creature.

Lifting her eyes to meet the Beast's, Belle was surprised to see that his were bright blue and almost human. Then the creature roared again.

Belle was at a loss. Her father would not allow her to take his place, but she could not leave him behind knowing he would soon perish in these conditions. Forced to make a terrible decision, she agreed to leave, but before she departed, Belle asked the Beast to allow her one last moment with her beloved father. The Beast didn't move. Belle cried, "Are you so cold-hearted that you won't allow a daughter to kiss her father goodbye? Forever can spare a minute!"

To her surprise, the Beast opened the prison door. Rushing inside, Belle embraced her father.

"I should have been with you," Belle said, hugging her father tightly.

Maurice tried to comfort his daughter, urging her to forget him and live her life. "I love you, Belle. Don't be afraid," he said.

"I'm not afraid," she whispered, her voice barely audible. "And I will escape, I promise."

Suddenly, Belle pushed her father out of the cell and slammed the door shut, locking herself inside. She had made her choice, and there was no going back. Belle's fate now sealed, the Beast dragged Maurice away and threw him out of the castle.

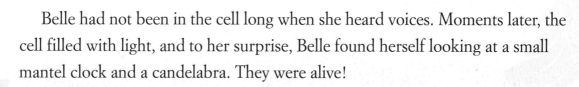

Belle had not been in the cell long when she heard voices. Moments later, the cell filled with light, and to her surprise, Belle found herself looking at a small mantel clock and a candelabra. They were alive!

"What are you?" she shouted in surprise.

"I am Lumiere," the candelabra replied, smiling broadly.

"And you can talk?" Belle asked.

"Of course he can talk," answered the mantel clock, whose name was Cogsworth.

As Belle watched, the two began to argue. It was only a moment before Lumiere took charge, to Cogsworth's dismay, and opened the cell door.

"Ready, miss?" he asked, pointing one of his candles towards the exit.

The odd pair led her back through the castle until they stopped in front of a huge set of doors. When the doors opened, Belle found herself looking at a beautiful bedroom. Up against one of the walls was a large wardrobe. Hearing the door open, it let out a very human-sounding snore and came to life. Belle was introduced to the wardrobe, Madame de Garderobe.

"Pretty eyes," the wardrobe said, eyeing Belle. "Proud face. Yes! I will find you something worthy of a princess."

The wardrobe began to pull out clothes willy-nilly. Before long, Belle was standing in the middle of the room in the most enormous and garish dress she had ever seen. It was clear to Belle that the castle staff was thrilled to have someone new in the castle, though each member had a different way of showing it.

Back in the village, Gaston was brooding. Even though he was sitting on his favourite chair in his favourite tavern, he was miserable. No one ever said no to Gaston. No one except Belle.

"There *are* other girls," LeFou pointed out to his friend. He nodded over his shoulder. A group of pretty girls sat in the corner, looking at Gaston hopefully.

Gaston barely noticed.

As Gaston's best friend, it was LeFou's job to cheer him up. Running around the tavern, LeFou got the villagers to pay Gaston compliments. No one was as great as Gaston; no one was as strong as Gaston; no one was as admired as Gaston. Gaston sighed. He had heard them all before. And of course, they were all true. He *was* exceptional.

So why, then, did Belle refuse to marry him? If only he had a way to change her mind – some leverage to make her say yes.

Just then, the door to the tavern flew open. Maurice stumbled inside. He was shaking and his clothing was torn.

"Help!" Maurice cried. "Somebody help me! We have to go ... not a minute to lose ..."

Gaston watched the old man. He looked crazy – his eyes were wild and he couldn't stop shaking.

"Whoa, whoa, whoa," the tavern keeper said. "Slow down, Maurice."

Maurice shook his head. "He's got Belle ... locked in a dungeon!"

Gaston sat up straighter, his interest piqued.

"Who's got her?" the tavern keeper asked.

"A beast!" Maurice answered. "A horrible, monstrous beast!"

Instantly, the tavern filled with laughter.

"This isn't a joke! His castle is hidden in the woods." Maurice stopped and looked around the room. "Will no one help me?"

As Gaston listened to the man ramble on, he had an idea. "I'll help you, Maurice," he said, getting to his feet. "Lead us to the Beast."

As they headed out of the tavern, Gaston smiled. He would help Maurice save Belle from the so-called Beast. Then she would have to marry him.

Inside the Beast's castle, Belle sat in her new room, feeling sad. She was all alone in a strange castle full of enchanted objects and she was sure she would never see her father or her home again. She was also very, very hungry.

Just then, there was a loud knock on her door. A moment later, she heard the Beast demand she join him for dinner.

"You've taken me prisoner and now you're asking me to dine with you?" Belle answered through the door. "Are you mad?"

That was not the right thing to say. She heard the Beast snarl, order his servants not to let her eat, and then storm away.

A lovely teapot named Mrs. Potts came to comfort her. She was the housekeeper of the estate. Luckily, the Beast's servants didn't always listen to their master. Before Belle knew what was happening, she found herself sitting at the head of a large dining room table. Lumiere led the plates, the cutlery, and the rest of the staff in a grand musical presentation of the most elaborate and delicious meal she had ever had.

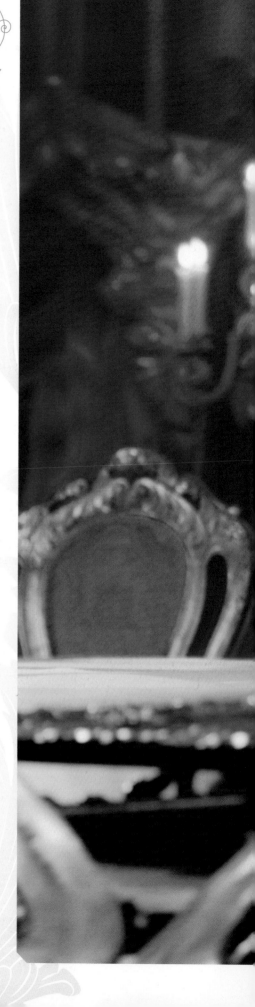

As Mrs. Potts led Belle back towards her room, Belle couldn't help asking, "Don't you ever want to escape?"

"The master's not as terrible as he appears," Mrs. Potts answered. "Somewhere deep in his soul, there's a prince of a fellow, just waiting to be set free."

Belle thought about asking what Mrs. Potts meant, but then her thoughts drifted to another mystery. "Lumiere mentioned something about the West Wing ..." she said.

Mrs. Potts shook her head. The West Wing was off-limits. She told Belle not to think about it and to go to sleep. Then she wished her good night and headed back to the kitchen.

Belle waited until Mrs. Potts had disappeared from view. Then she glanced up at the stairs in front of her. If she went left, she would continue back to her room. But if she went right ... She gazed up the set of stairs as she made up her mind. Taking a deep breath, she started to climb towards the West Wing.

Soon Belle found herself walking down a long, dark hallway. At the end of the hallway was a single door. It had been left open.

Her curiosity growing, Belle opened the door further and walked into a large room. It was clearly the Beast's suite. On the floor was a nest of a bed: crumpled blankets, torn bits of hay and ripped fabric. The walls had been slashed by deep claw marks. In one corner, a portrait of a royal family lay, ripped apart; the only feature left untouched was a pair of bright blue eyes that reminded her of the Beast's.

As Belle turned away from the painting, her attention was caught by a table standing in front of the balcony doors. Atop the table was a beautiful glass jar. Inside, a single red rose hung magically in the air.

Mesmerised, Belle reached out her hand. Her fingertips grazed the etched glass. *"What are you doing here?"*

The Beast's roar scared Belle. Looking over, she saw him appear out of the shadows.

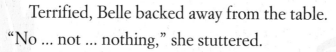

Terrified, Belle backed away from the table. "No ... not ... nothing," she stuttered.

"Do you realise what you could have done?" the Beast snarled. One of his arms hit a thin column causing it to crumble, pieces falling close to the glass jar. Panic filled the Beast's eyes. He threw his body over the rose to shield it, screaming, *"Get out!"*

Belle ran. But the enchanted servants tried their best not to let her leave. For one moment Belle was worried she was trapped ... again. Then she saw Froufrou, a little dog who had become a piano bench, race past her and out through a small door. Before anyone or anything could stop her, she slipped out the same way. Moments later, she was racing away from the castle as fast as Philippe could take her.

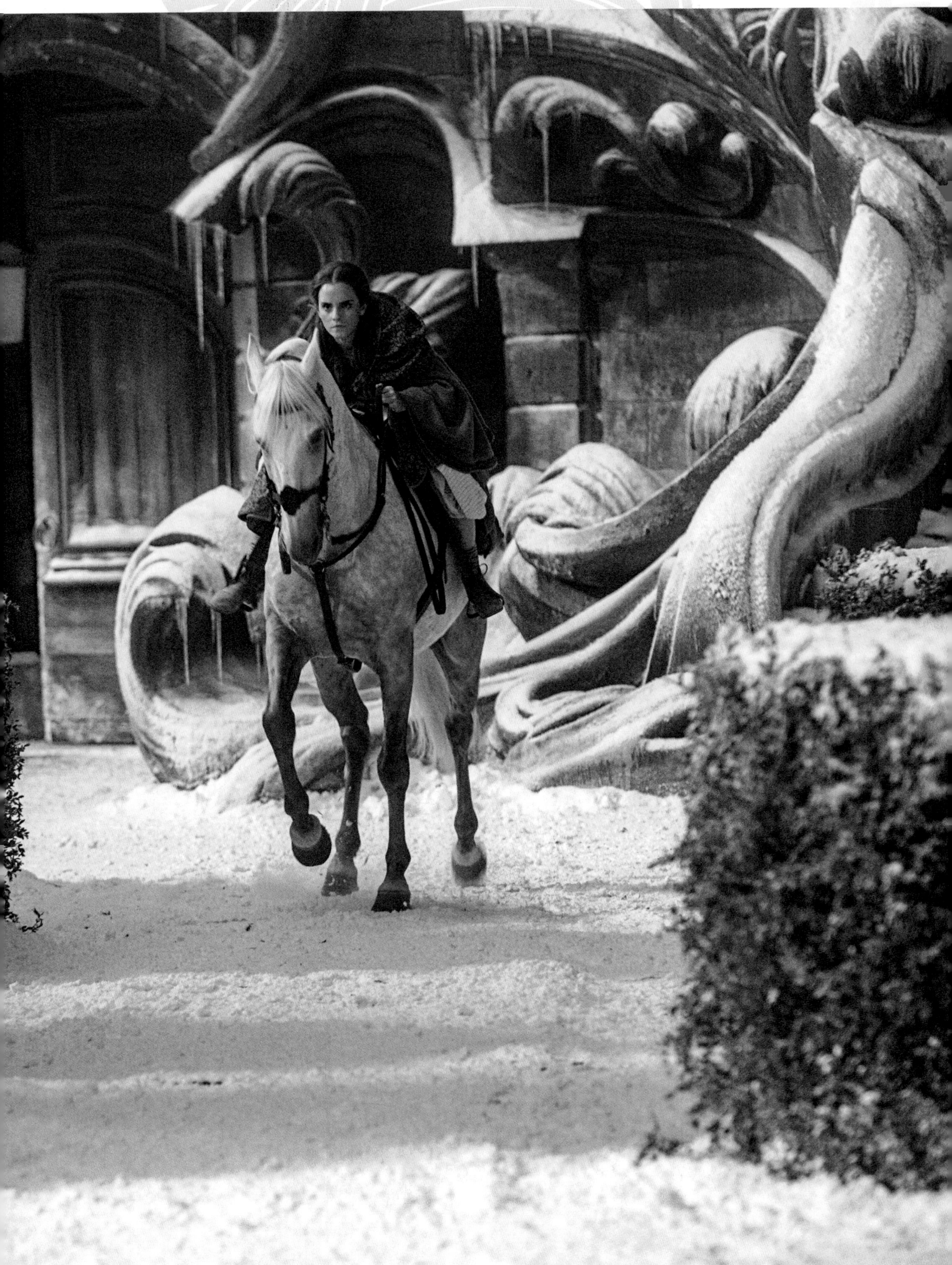

Belle and Philippe hadn't gone far when they heard wolves howling. Looking over her shoulder, Belle saw the hungry animals chasing Philippe.

A moment later, the horse raced onto a frozen pond.

There was a loud creaking noise as the ice began to crack under the horse's weight. Philippe bucked, keeping the wolves' snapping jaws from closing on his legs. Belle leapt onto a snow bank and fought off the vicious animals as best she could, but they began to close in around her. Suddenly, as if from nowhere, the Beast appeared.

The Beast jumped into the middle of the wolf pack. Snarling and snapping his powerful teeth, he fought them one by one. He was bigger than the wolves, but the Beast was outnumbered. Then, with a burst of strength, he threw the biggest wolf to the ground. Seeing their leader hurt, the others took off running.

Safe, Belle turned to leave. But when she glanced over her shoulder, she noticed the Beast had collapsed to the ground, hurt badly from the fight. She paused. He had just saved her life.

Belle knew the only thing – the right thing – to do was help him. With difficulty, the Beast stood and Belle helped him onto Philippe's back. Then they began the long, slow walk back to the castle.

In another part of the forest, Gaston was beginning to think that Maurice really *was* crazy. They had been riding through the woods for hours and had not seen a castle yet.

"Maurice, enough is enough," Gaston said, turning to look at the older man. "We have to turn back."

But Belle's father wasn't ready to give up. "Look! That is the tree!" Maurice exclaimed. The tree, he told Gaston and LeFou, marked the entrance to the enchanted forest. The castle had to be close by!

Gaston's eyes narrowed. He was trying very hard not to lose his temper, but the old man was making it difficult. "There are no such things as beasts, or talking teacups, or ... whatever."

Maurice looked at Gaston in confusion. "If you didn't believe me, why did you offer to help?" he asked.

"Because I want to marry your daughter," Gaston said, with no attempt to hide his plan any longer. "Now let's go home."

"I told you! She's not at home, she's with the —"

"If you say 'beast' one more time, I will feed you to the wolves!" Gaston screamed.

Gaston's behaviour was not lost on Maurice. "Captain," he said, backing up a step, "now that I've seen your true face, you'll *never* marry my daughter."

Gaston pulled back his arm and hit Maurice, knocking him unconscious.

"If Maurice won't give me his blessing," Gaston said, picking up the older man and carrying him to a tree, "then he is in my way."

He pulled a rope out of the carriage and tied Maurice to the tree. "Once the wolves are finished with him, Belle will have no one to take care of her but *me*."

Without a second glance, Gaston climbed back into the carriage and turned towards home.

Upstairs in the castle, the Beast was proving to be a terrible patient. Ever since Belle had taken him back to the castle, he had been cranky.

"That hurts!" he snarled, as Belle tried to clean one of his cuts.

"If you held still, it wouldn't hurt as much," Belle said, grabbing his arm and yanking it towards her.

"If *you* hadn't run away," the Beast said, his jaw clenched, "this wouldn't have happened."

"Well, if you hadn't frightened me, I wouldn't have run away!" Belle retorted.

"Well, you shouldn't have been in the West Wing!" the Beast countered angrily.

"Well, you should learn to control your temper," Belle said. And with that, the Beast was still. Belle had made her point.

As the Beast drifted off to sleep, Belle turned to leave. To her surprise, she saw that Lumiere and Mrs. Potts had been watching them the whole time.

"Why do you care so much about him?" Belle asked softly. "He's cursed you somehow."

In response, Mrs. Potts began to tell her the Beast's story. Once, the Beast had been just a little boy who loved his mother with all his heart. Back then, the castle had been a happier place. But the boy's mother became gravely ill and passed away.

Nothing was ever the same after that. All he was left with was his father, who was cruel at heart and shaped his son in his image. The castle grew dark and cold and so did the boy's heart. And then ... the Enchantress cursed him.

As Mrs. Potts finished her story, Belle's eyes fell on the glass jar. Inside, the rose was fading.

"What happens when the last petal falls?" she asked softly.

"The master remains a beast forever," Lumiere replied. "And the rest of us become ..."

"Antiques," Mrs. Potts finished. Then, with a heavy sigh, she turned and left the room. A moment later, Lumiere followed.

Belle's heart grew heavy for her new friends. She wished there were something she could do to help.

For the next few days, Belle remained by the Beast's side, watching over him as he slept, doing whatever she could to help him heal. While she passed the hours in silence, Belle's mind drifted until she found herself reciting lines from a Shakespeare play aloud. To her surprise, the Beast awoke at the sound of her voice, finishing the lines as she spoke them.

"You know Shakespeare?" she asked.

Belle discovered the Beast was in fact well educated and quite the bookworm, almost as much as she was. When Belle told the Beast that her favourite work of Shakespeare's was *Romeo and Juliet*, the Beast teasingly scoffed and said there were so many better things to read than tragic romances.

Intrigued, Belle asked, "Like what?" And with that, he led her to the most amazing place she had yet seen.

Belle gasped. Beyond a huge set of doors was an enormous library. There were thousands of books. They lined the walls, the tables and even the mantelpiece. Several big, comfortable-looking chairs were placed around the room. It was Belle's dream come true.

"It's wonderful," she said softly.

"You think so?" the Beast asked, sounding oddly happy. "Then it's yours. You can be master here." He turned to go.

Taken aback by his surprising generosity, Belle asked, "Have you really read every one of these books?"

The Beast stopped and considered her question. "Not all of them," he replied. "Some are in Greek."

"Was that a joke?" Belle asked, beginning to smile. "Are you making jokes now?"

"Maybe ..." the Beast said, hiding his own smile.

As the days passed, Belle realised that something had changed between her and the Beast. They were almost becoming friends.

She and the Beast now ate their meals together. When the weather was nice, they walked around the castle grounds together. When the weather wasn't so nice, they had snowball fights.

Belle no longer shuddered if the Beast accidently touched her with his paw. And she was no longer scared of his fangs when he smiled.

The new friendship was not lost on Lumiere, Cogsworth, or Mrs. Potts. They watched Belle and the Beast happily. Maybe the curse was not as unbreakable as it had seemed.

As Belle and the Beast continued to get to know each other, they spoke of the small village where Belle had grown up. She shared with him that she often felt like an outsider there. The Beast understood her feelings all too well. A thought came to his mind and he asked Belle if she'd like to run away with him. The question intrigued her, even more so when he showed her a large leather-bound book in the library. It was an enchanted volume with special powers.

He placed her hands with his on top of the book. "Think of the place you've most wanted to see. First, see it in your mind's eye. Now feel it in your heart."

Belle closed her eyes.

When she opened them, they were no longer in the Beast's castle. They were in Paris. Belle was standing in the apartment she had lived in with her father and mother. It looked abandoned.

"What happened to your mother?" the Beast asked gently.

"That's the only story Papa could never bring himself to tell," Belle said.

The Beast's eyes travelled around the room, finally settling on a black mask with a bird-like nose, tucked away in a corner. The mask was a sign of plague, doctors had worn them to keep from getting sick themselves. With this discovery, Belle knew the answer to the question she had never dared ask.

Wiping tears from her eyes, Belle took one last look around the room. She had seen enough. "Let's go home," she said, taking the Beast's hand.

It had been five days since Gaston had left Maurice tied up in the woods. LeFou was beginning to worry, but Maurice had not returned to tell the tale. As Gaston strode confidently into the tavern, he was sure he was free and clear, until he saw an unexpected guest in the middle of the room surrounded by a crowd. It was Maurice!

"Gaston," one of the men said when he saw him. "Did you try to kill Maurice?"

Gaston pretended to be offended. "Oh, Maurice," he said. "Thank heavens. I've spent the last five days trying to find you. Why did you run off into the forest in your condition?"

Maurice shook his head. "No! You tried to kill me! You left me for the wolves!"

Gaston raised an eyebrow. He would never do such a thing, he told the villagers.

To Gaston's surprise, Pere Robert, the village priest, stepped in front of Maurice defensively. "Listen to me, all of you," he said to the crowd. "This is Maurice, our neighbour. Our friend. He is a good man."

"Are you suggesting that I am not?" Gaston said, feigning hurt at the suggestion.

The villagers began to mumble among themselves, their doubt about Maurice growing.

"Maurice," Jean the potter said, turning to look at the old man, "do you have any proof of what you're saying?"

Unfortunately, Maurice had little proof. He said the village beggar, Agathe, had freed him and could confirm his claim, but Gaston quickly discounted her as a lowly, filthy hag. When Maurice called upon LeFou to tell the truth of what had happened, LeFou could not bring himself to slander his best friend, Gaston.

Gaston smirked. Once again, he was in control. "Maurice, it pains me to say this," Gaston said, "but you've become a danger to yourself and others. You need help, sir. A place to heal your troubled mind."

Turning, he nodded to two men standing in the corner. They stepped forward and grabbed Maurice by the arms. Then they began to drag him out of the tavern.

Gaston told the villagers not to worry. He would make *sure* Maurice was safe. By Gaston's arrangement, Maurice would be taken to an insane asylum. Now nothing was standing in the way of Gaston marrying Belle.

At the castle, there was a frenzy of activity as the staff helped prepare the Beast to share a romantic evening with Belle. After their trip to Paris, the Beast was sure he loved her. The only problem was that he wasn't sure she loved him in return. He was hoping he would find out that night.

"Do not be discouraged," Lumiere said to the Beast, as he got ready. The servants were all helping him. "She is the one."

"She deserves so much more than a beast," the Beast responded.

Mrs. Potts shook her head. "We love you," she said. "So stop being a coward and tell Belle how you feel."

As Belle finished dressing, she could hardly believe her eyes. She was wearing the most beautiful gown, adorned with sparkling gold dust. This would be a night unlike any she had experienced before.

Taking a deep breath, Belle picked up the front of her dress and left her room. Reaching the staircase, she looked down. To her surprise, the Beast was standing at the bottom of the stairs. Both seemed a little nervous. Walking side by side, they entered the magnificent ballroom.

Music filled the air, and beneath the glow of candlelit crystal chandeliers, Belle and the Beast danced together beautifully.

As the lights dimmed, they walked out onto the large terrace connected to the ballroom. Belle looked up at the starry sky.

"I haven't danced in years," the Beast said after a moment. "I'd almost forgotten the feeling." He looked down at Belle. His gaze was full of warmth. Then he spoke again. "It's foolish, I suppose, for a creature like me to hope that one day he might earn your affection."

Belle thought for a second before she spoke. "Can anyone be happy if they aren't free?" she said. The Beast was struck by her meaningful words. Then Belle said, "My father taught me to dance."

The Beast could see that Belle missed her father very much. He wanted to make her feel better, so he took her back to the West Wing and held up a small mirror. The mirror would show the viewer anything he or she wanted to see. Belle said, "I would like to see my father."

The face of the mirror began to swirl magically. Then Maurice appeared. Belle gasped as she saw her father being dragged through the village square. He looked scared.

"Papa!" she cried. "What are they doing to him?"

The Beast's eyes grew wide as he, too, saw what was happening to the old man. As Belle continued to watch her father through the mirror, the Beast's gaze shifted to the rose jar.

Inside, another petal dropped.

The Beast knew what he had to do.

"You must go to him," he said.

Belle didn't know what to say. The Beast had just released her. She should have been happy, but instead, the moment was bittersweet. Softly, she thanked him, and she moved to return the mirror. The Beast shook his head. He wanted her to keep it so she could always look back on him.

Before Belle could change her mind, she turned and ran out of the room.

The Beast watched as Belle raced into the stable, saddled Philippe and disappeared into the woods. The Beast sighed. The last petal would fall from the rose soon, and when that happened, he would remain a beast forever.

When Belle arrived at the village, she found a crowd gathered in the square. It seemed every villager had come to watch Maurice be thrown into the horse-drawn carriage marked with the word *asylum*.

"Stop!" Belle cried.

Everyone turned. Seeing Belle, still in her golden ball gown, they began to whisper to one another.

Belle ignored them. "My father's not crazy!" she protested. Spotting Gaston, Belle called to him, "Gaston ... tell them!"

But to her surprise, Gaston did not take her side. "Your father *has* been making some unbelievable claims," he said.

"It's true," another villager said. "He's been raving about a beast in a castle."

"But I have just come from the castle," Belle said quickly. "There *is* a beast!"

Her hand closed around the mirror. "You want proof?" she asked loudly. She pulled out the mirror and held it up. *"Show me the Beast!"*

Once again, the mirror face began to swirl magically, until it revealed the Beast. He was slumped against the cold grey stone of the castle.

Seeing the Beast, the villagers gasped in fright. Belle grew worried. She thought showing the Beast would help save her father. But instead, it had put the Beast in danger.

"Don't be afraid," she said. "He's gentle and kind."

"She is clearly under a spell," Gaston cried. "If I didn't know better, I'd say she even *cared* for this monster."

It didn't take long for Gaston to convince the villagers that they needed to go to the castle and destroy the Beast. Within moments, the once peaceful villagers had become an angry mob.

Belle knew she had to get to the castle to warn the Beast. But Gaston had Belle thrown into the asylum cart with Maurice. Then, with the angry mob following him, he led the charge towards the Beast's castle.

Inside the cart, Belle thought frantically of how they might escape. Belle told her father that the Beast truly was kind and not the monster he had first seen. Maurice believed his daughter and resolved to pick the lock on the cart doors using Belle's hair pin.

Moments later, Belle was racing Philippe back towards the Beast's castle. She only hoped she would get there in time to stop Gaston and save the Beast.

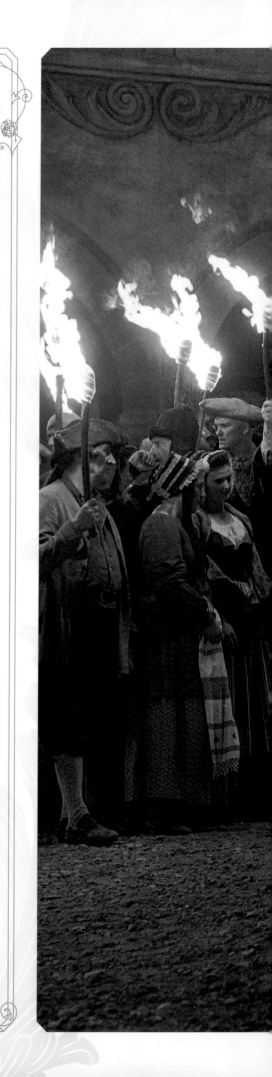

Inside the castle, the staff had gathered together. They were heartbroken that Belle had left. Like the Beast, they knew she had been their last chance to break the curse. Now it seemed they would never return to their human form.

Hearing something outside, the staff peered out the windows. Seeing the light from a dozen torches coming closer, they knew they were in danger. Luckily, Lumiere had a plan. They would act like what they were – household objects. That would give them the element of surprise.

Quickly, the staff got into position. They waited until the villagers had all filed into the foyer. Then Mrs. Potts gave the order. *"Attack!"* she shouted.

The villagers didn't know what hit them. One minute they had been in a room full of an odd assortment of furniture, and the next minute that furniture was attacking them. The villagers shrieked in fear and began to flee.

While the other villagers ran out of the castle, Gaston proceeded up the stairs. He intended to find the Beast and kill him.

He ran down one hallway after another until he spotted the Beast, who was standing on a balcony. Pulling out his gun, Gaston approached the Beast. "Were you in love with her?" he asked.

The Beast said nothing. Instead, he turned his back to Gaston.

Gaston fired his gun.

Just as the Beast dropped over the side of the balcony, Gaston prepared to fire again, this time with his crossbow. But when he reached for an arrow, there were none in his quiver. He turned to find Belle had taken them, snapping them all in half.

Having finally reached the castle, Belle had run immediately upstairs. Now, she stared down Gaston.

"You prefer that misshapen thing to me ... when I offered you everything?" he asked in disbelief.

Belle cringed. The man standing in front of her was far more of a beast than the Beast.

"When we return to the village, you will marry me," Gaston snarled. "And the Beast's head will hang on our wall!"

"Never!" Belle shouted.

Gaston swung through a window in the turret, following the Beast's movements as Belle tried to get to the Beast. He lost his gun in the process. Gaston saw that the Beast had survived his fall and was climbing slowly back towards Belle.

"Fight me, Beast!" Gaston shouted when he caught up. He began to hit him with a stone club. Under the combined weight of Gaston and the Beast, the footbridge began to crumble. But Gaston's attention was elsewhere, he had spotted his fallen rifle.

"Gaston! *No!*" Belle's cry warned the Beast. Just in time, he turned to see Gaston, who was about to strike him once more. The Beast reached up and yanked the stone weapon from Gaston's hands. Then he wrapped his paw around Gaston's throat and swung him off the edge of the crumbling footbridge.

"No," Gaston pleaded, as his legs dangled over open air. "Please. Don't hurt me, Beast. I'll do anything."

For a long moment, the Beast just stared at Gaston, his features twisted with rage and hate. Then his gaze met Belle's. He wanted to be the man she saw, not the Beast he had become. Slowly, he swung Gaston back over the bridge's wall and set him down.

"Go," he said. "Get out."

As Gaston scrambled away, the Beast dropped down on all fours and began to run towards the edge of the footbridge. He jumped.

As his front feet landed on the balcony, the Beast smiled. He had made it back to Belle ...

Boom! The Beast let out a roar of agony, as the sound of gunfire echoed over the castle.

As Belle screamed, Gaston reloaded the rifle. *Boom!* He fired again. The bullet flew through the air and slammed into the Beast. He fell to the ground.

But Gaston's luck, it would seem, had just run out. The stones beneath his feet crumbled. In an instant, there was only empty air beneath him and a long drop into nothingness.

Belle rushed to the Beast's side. Falling to her knees, she gently lifted his head into her lap.

When the Beast felt her touch, his eyes opened. "You came back," he said.

"Of course I came back," she said, trying not to cry. "I'll never leave you again."

The Beast sighed. "I'm afraid it's my turn to leave," he said, his voice weak.

The Beast's head grew heavier. Belle looked down at him, tears flowing from her eyes. They had shared so much and grown together in ways Belle had never thought were possible. From a menacing and threatening captor, he had become a kind and kindred soul. And now he was taking his last breaths.

Belle choked back a sob. "We're together now," she said. "It's going to be fine. You'll see."

"At least I got to see you one last time," the Beast said. Then his eyes closed. His breathing grew slower. And finally, it stopped.

The Beast was gone.

On a terrace below, unaware of the fate that had just befallen their master, the staff of the castle was celebrating. They had kept the castle safe.

As Lumiere turned to congratulate his old friend Cogsworth, his candles dimmed. The clock was moving oddly. In fact, he was barely moving at all.

One by one, each member of the staff became lifeless, until Lumiere was the only one left.

Soon the terrace was quiet except for the ticking of the clock that had once been Cogsworth. A soft snow began to fall.

The last petal had fallen. The curse was taking effect. Belle stared down at the Beast. His blue eyes were closed and she brushed her palm over his cheek. "Please, don't leave me. Come back," she begged.

Belle leaned over and placed a soft kiss on his forehead. And then, ever so gently, she whispered, "I love you."

Instantly, a change began to take place. Belle watched in disbelief as the Beast's body slowly rose into the air and transformed back into a human. He landed softly on his feet, next to Belle.

Belle slowly approached him. In silent disbelief, she ran a finger through the Prince's hair and looked into his blue eyes. *It was him.* Smiling, they leaned towards each other and kissed.

Throughout the castle, the curse gave up its hold. The sun shone, turning the stormy sky a brilliant blue. The cold grey stone walls became a warm gold and the snow gave way to bright green grass. After so long, everything was coming back to life, including the staff.

Lumiere's candles turned back into arms, while Cogsworth's clock hands transformed into a moustache. Mrs. Potts was no longer a teapot but the castle's housekeeper once more. The castle soon filled with the sounds of laughter.

Belle and the Prince joined the happy crowd and were surrounded by their friends with hugs and cheers.

Belle, the Prince, the castle staff and all their loved ones from the village celebrated this joyous time with a grand ball.

Dancing across the floor, Belle knew she could never be happier. She was surrounded by her family – old and new. Maurice was there, smiling as he watched his daughter twirl. Lumiere, Cogsworth and Mrs. Potts were there, as well. All was finally just as it should be.

As Belle lifted her eyes, her gaze met the Prince's. She loved him more with each passing day. And as they danced to the music, they knew that their tale would end as all tales should ... *happily ever after*.